The Christmas tree stands at the very center of the action during the holidays. It lights the way through the dark, guards the gifts, brings joy.

But once the holidays end and the needles fall, the owners kick the trees to the curb. Quite literally.

Which is where I find them.

I listen to their stories, good or bad. And help them transition into the next phase of their existence.

A Second Chance is a fantasy post-Christmas story about letting go of the past and finding new beginnings.

R.W. WALLACE

AUTHOR OF *MORBIER IMPOSSIBLE*

A Second Chance

A Holiday Short Story

A Second Chance
by R.W. Wallace

Copyright © 2020 by R.W. Wallace

Cover by the author
Copy edit by Wendy Janes
Cover Illustration 101247885 © Amethystgraphics | Dreamstime.com
Cover Illustration 24115157 © eriksvoboda | 123rf.com

All characters and events in this book, other than those clearly in the public domain, are fictitious and any resemblance to real persons, living or dead, is purely coincidental.

All rights reserved. No part of this publication may be reproduced, distributed, or transmitted in any form or by any means, including photocopying, recording, or other electronic or mechanical methods, without the prior written permission of the publisher, except in the case of brief quotations embodied in critical reviews and certain other noncommercial uses permitted by copyright law. For permission requests, write to the publisher, addressed "Attention: Permissions Coordinator," at the address below.

www.rwwallace.com

ISBN: [979-10-95707-52-3]

Main category—Fiction
Other category—Fantasy

First Edition

14 13 12 11 10 / 10 9 8 7 6 5 4 3 2 1

Also by R.W. Wallace

Mystery

The Tolosa Mystery Series
The Red Brick Haze (free)
The Red Brick Cellars
The Red Brick Basilica

Ghost Detective Shorts
Just Desserts
Lost Friends
Family Bonds
Common Ground

Short Stories
Hidden Horrors
Cold Blue Eternity
Critters
Gertrude and the Trojan Horse
First Impressions
Let Them Eat Cake
Out of Sight
Two's Company
Like Mother Like Daughter

Science Fiction (short stories)
The Vanguard
Quarantine
Common Enemies

Fantasy
Morbier Impossible
Unexpected Consequences

A Second Chance

Everybody loves a good Christmas tree for Christmas. But once the holidays are over, the trees must go. Nobody wants an old skeleton with twisted limbs and hardly any needles left, standing in the middle of their living room, reminding them that the party's over. So before they go back to work, back to school, back to their everyday lives, they remove the pretty decorations, take down the lights, remove the bright star, and throw the tree out.

Nobody cares what becomes of them.

Most of the time, if they can get away with it, they'll dump the tree anywhere. Even some families who have a fireplace don't go through the trouble of cutting up the tree for firewood. They prefer the wood they bought at the store, which is the right size, and isn't sticky, and won't soil their fireplace. And won't require any physical labor on their part.

In the countryside, the trees that aren't used for firewood usually end up in a ditch, or in the forest, looking up at their living siblings, as they waste away.

In the city, where the risk of getting caught for littering is much greater, most trees are lucky enough to be deposited in a place that will allow them to be recycled.

A place like this.

I stand guard in front of the City Hall, watching over the dying Christmas trees. It is two days before the end of the school holidays, and high season for throwing away Christmas trees.

The city has dozens of these stations, spread out in different neighborhoods and suburbs, in the hopes that people will go to the trouble of bringing their trees. We know from experience that they will not bring them to the waste collection.

Yesterday I brought back over a hundred and fifty trees. From the looks of it, today we'll go over two hundred.

I approach a large fir tree which is leaning against the wooden fence we've set up. She's almost two meters high and has perfect proportions. Her branches still have all their needles, standing to attention. She has no wood boards nailed to her trunk, or signs of having been screwed into a tree stand. The last ten centimeters of the trunk is slightly darkened. She's been allowed a flowerpot, to continue the semblance of life while she served her family.

A Second Chance

I brush the fingers of one hand lightly across the needles.

Christmas presents going way above the lower limbs. Two types of white lights; fake candles and falling snow. *Foie gras*, snails in their delicious buttery sauce, beef, potatoes, the traditional *bûche*, and an apple sorbet *trou Normand*—in Armagnac.

I smile at the fir. "You got a good one, huh?"

I lean in and take a good sniff. She smells of wood smoke, long family dinners, and children's laughter. No yelling about going to bed, only long hugs and sweet kisses. No lack of anything, including love.

This fir has lived every Christmas tree's wet dream.

I walk farther down the fence to a pine tree with several broken branches and very few needles left. The pines are usually quite resistant and rarely lose their needles, even after being used as a decoration for over four weeks.

"What happened to you, babe?" I whisper as I trace my hand along one of the broken branches stripped of needles.

Two boys fighting. One probably five years old. The other closer to ten. They're pulling on a fireman's truck, the smallest boy screaming that it's his, his older brother claiming that he can use it as long as his brother isn't playing with it.

The mother coming through the door as the boys crash into the tree. *What are you doing!* she screams at them, her hands coming up, vibrating, next to her head, as if she's resisting tearing out her hair. *Why can't you get along for two minutes? Why do you have to ruin everything?*

The boys, silent in the face of their mother's onslaught, scramble away from the toppled tree. The oldest attempts to straighten the broken branch, but the limb falls down, pointing to the ground.

The fire truck is long forgotten.

You ruined the tree! The boys scoot away as the mother stalks to the trembling pine.

She straightens the branch in much the same way her son has just attempted. When it falls down, she yanks at it, needles falling to the floor. More pulling. *If you can't stay up, you can just get lost.*

But no amount of pulling would break the branch all the way off. So they end up turning the tree to hide the ugly branch in the corner.

Of course, that only worked the first time.

I lean in for a sniff. At least the boys got lots of presents, and not many that they needed to share.

I give the tree a pat. "Don't you worry. You did your job well. And you're not done yet. I'm sure you'll love what we have in store for you."

The bells of the Basilica of Saint-Sernin Basilica ring eight o'clock and I tell my colleague with the large truck to collect the trees. I help him move all the trees into the waiting truck, taking a couple of seconds for each to listen to their stories, giving an encouraging word where it's needed.

Officially, my work ends here. I'm only supposed to collect the trees that people bring me.

But these aren't the trees that really need rescuing.

I get into my little truck and ease down the narrow streets in the direction of the canal.

This is not my first time playing; I know where the lost ones go.

The truck is narrow enough to be able to drive on the cycling path along the canal. I just need to use my key to remove one of the barriers, and off we go.

I don't have to go far before I find the first one. He seems to be a spruce, though it's difficult to tell since only his lower branches and trunk are above water.

Easing out of the driver's seat, I call out to him. "Don't you worry, honey. I'll get you out."

The poor thing is only a meter or so from the edge of the canal, so I grab a pole with a hook on the end to drag it toward me.

He's a small one. Large and wide branches at the base, but his top doesn't even reach my shoulders. He has clearly been kept up by nailing two planks to his base, but the planks have been removed, leaving only four tiny holes where the nails went in. The branches and needles are in relatively good shape. All in all, he seems healthy. For a tree doomed to die, that is.

I prop the little thing up against the back of my truck and remove my gloves. Shoving them into my back pocket, I reach out to caress the crown.

A crooked star drawn on paper and glued to a piece of cardboard. A metal wire shoved through the star's center and coiled around the very top of the tree. The lines are uneven and the coloring full of holes—the creator can't be more than six years old.

One branch seems to have lost more needles than the others. I lean down to inspect it.

With the smell of tree, and water, and woodsmoke, comes the image of a little girl with long dark hair decorating the tree all by herself. She puts almost all the decorations on this one branch, admiring how pretty it becomes for each item she adds. After a comment—a female voice coming from across the room, apparently from the couch—she adds a few decorations to two or three other branches. But all the while the tree stands in the living room, the little girl only admires this favorite branch.

I inspect other areas of the little spruce, looking for signs of the parents. But I find only the little girl taking care of her tree.

Finally, I lift the tree into the trunk of my truck and put my hand on the base. This is where most people grab the tree when they need to transport it anywhere, especially when it no longer needs to stay pretty.

There she is.

A skinny woman in her early thirties, with long dark, matted hair, dragging the tree behind her as she shuffles along the cycling path by the canal.

Her intention was to go to the Christmas tree round-up where I work.

People are looking at her. Noticing the state of her hair, her clothes. And she's cold. So cold. She should be home in her bed, cuddled into her corner of the couch. Maybe a cup of tea, some chocolate. And her daughter's sweet smiles.

This reminds her of going to work. She used to walk this way to get to the train station. Back in the days when she managed to get out of bed and do something constructive with her time.

She'd get back someday. When she was better.

When she is halfway across the pedestrian bridge crossing the canal, she gives up on her mission and lets the little tree drop into the murky waters below when no one is looking.

The little spruce, only his trunk out of the water, watches his hostess shuffle home to give her daughter a kiss.

"Mmm," I hum to the tree as I make sure he's secure at the back of my truck. "Looks like you had a bit of a challenge, huh? Don't you worry though. You did a great job. You hold onto the memories of your little girl being happy taking care of her Christmas tree. And know that there was clearly lots of love in their household."

Head down, I enter the truck's cab and start the engine. I wish there was something I could do for the woman, but my powers only stretch so far. I'll have to satisfy myself with taking care of the trees, like I always do.

I continue my rounds for a couple of hours, picking up twelve trees from various sidewalks, alleys, and trash cans.

I listen to their stories, tell them they did a good job, and that I have a new task for them.

It's just as I decide to stop for the day that I find the little alien.

I've done this for eight years now, and this has never happened before. I know they exist, of course. Who doesn't. But they don't usually end up on the sidewalk with their living siblings.

He's made of plastic, but the quality is good enough to make him seem lifelike. He's not even perfectly symmetrical, and not because he's been used, but because he was produced that way. He looks like he's covered in snow, but that's also fake, naturally.

He stands here on a street corner, almost as if he's part of the city's Christmas decorations. He stands straight, and is positioned exactly on the corner between two small streets.

I leave my truck behind and approach cautiously. Will this work?

I flick one plastic fake-snow-covered needle with my index finger.

Silence.

I don't always get sound through the visions, but this isn't an absence of sound.

It's a loud, heavy, gray silence. The kind that comes from screaming inside your head. The kind that covers your heart and suffocates it.

I see no decorations, so I move to caress a branch on the opposite side of the tree.

Still nothing. There's a vague memory of lights and angels and shimmering balls, but it's faint, probably from last year. With it comes the image of a man and a woman, slow-dancing without music in front of their tree, the remains of a large meal on the kitchen table.

As I continue easing my hands over the branches, I'm starting to make out some recent surroundings—impressions are more difficult to drag out through the plastic than through living wood, but they're there. He's standing in the corner of the living room, not in the center like he did the year before.

Right next to him: a large cardboard box full of Christmas ornaments.

They never left the box this year.

Most trees give off a whiff of feelings, carried on their scent. To understand them, all one needs to do is not think with words, but with feelings. Let the heart take over from the brain.

This fellow doesn't have a scent, not one his own anyway. But I'm still hearing him, loud and clear.

Sadness. Loss. Frustration.

"What happened, hon? Why didn't you get a Christmas this year?"

Using all my powers and taking my time, I manage to pull the story out of him.

He'd heard them all through the four seasons, from up in the attic—his home for forty-eight weeks of the year.

It started with the woman crying in February. Inconsolable crying for an entire week. Anything could set her off; her husband going grocery shopping, being invited to visit friends, hearing the neighbors reprimanding their kids as they passed in front of the house.

The husband did his best, really. *We'll be all right, honey. We'll try again, and it'll work in no time, you'll see. Why don't we go visit your sister, maybe that'll cheer you up? Of course she won't gloat! Is that really what you think of your only sister?*

Nothing helped, and as the days turned into weeks, the husband's tone slowly went from soothing and sad to something close to accusing and frustrated.

Are you trying to tell me it's my *fault? Because this hurt me just as much as it hurt you, you know. But I'm willing to move on.*

The wife snapped out of her sadness then. To move straight into anger. *Willing to move on, my ass. You're just willing to get laid.*

And on they went, their barbs hitting closer and closer to the heart, and with increasing frequency.

It took a turn for the worse in August. The husband was away for a week on a business trip when the wife learned of her sister's pregnancy.

She'd not made it to work that week, and managed to alienate most of her family. The little tree heard her on the phone with her cousins and her parents, explaining that her sister had gotten knocked up only to spite her.

Since none of them knew of what had happened in February, they hung up on her. She spent an entire night crying on the floor in the living room, never making it to the bedroom.

When the husband came home, he noticed nothing different.

They only communicated when strictly necessary; to ask the other to take out the trash, or to ask what was for dinner, or to inform of an office party they both needed to attend.

The wife told her husband about her sister's happy news two weeks later. As far as the tree could discern, she hadn't had uninterrupted sleep for more than an hour or two since the last phone call.

I told you about her, she yelled at her husband. *I told you she was evil. Now she's gotten pregnant just to spite me.*

To spite you? Really? You can't even envision her doing it for herself, because it's what she wants for her life? You can't identify with that at all? Really? Who's the father? Is she still with that Matthieu fellow?

Something crashed to the floor, possibly a plate or a mug. *Why can't you ever take my side in anything? What did I ever do to you?*

You're treating me like I don't even exist, that's what! You're ignoring the fact that I'm suffering too. You've retreated into your little bubble and won't ever let me in.

A long silence followed. For the tree, who was used to waiting and not doing anything for months at a time, it was quick, but for humans, it must have been excruciating.

I think you should see someone, he finally said. *A professional. I don't know how to help you on my own.*

She hadn't had an answer to that. In fact, the tree heard not a sound from her for several weeks. They both opened and closed doors, heated water in the kettle, and flushed the toilet. She was obviously there, since her husband talked to her, in a tone of voice usually reserved for mortal enemies, but she never replied or spoke back.

Then, the first week of December, only thirty minutes after the husband had pulled the poor tree down from the attic, and prepared the box of decorations, she spoke again.

I'm leaving.

The tree was out of the dusty attic, finally able to see, but there was nothing *to* see. The wife never came back, and the husband came home from work late at night only to go straight to bed.

This morning, hair about three weeks overdue for a haircut, bags the size of pine cones under his eyes, and breath coming unevenly, the husband had dropped the box of Christmas decorations in the trash and dumped the tree on a street corner on his way to work.

I sigh. "You poor thing," I tell the tree. "You know there was nothing you could do, right?"

I glance back at my truck, its bed filled with abandoned trees. *Real* trees. Which I know what to do with, to give them a new purpose.

But what do I do with a plastic tree?

The glimmer of an idea appears in my mind. In any case, there's no way I can just leave the poor thing here on the street.

The next morning, I'm unloading my catch from the day before at a sawmill some fifty kilometers outside of Toulouse.

"Here we are, my beauties," I say as I line up the trees next to my truck, to give them a clear view of the premises.

"Now, I realize this looks mighty scary. But I'm here to help. Now." I point at the main entrance. "In there is where we're going to cut off the branches."

I'm walking down the line of trees with my hand out, so I can listen to them all in quick succession as I give them my speech. I never try to sugarcoat this part. It's not pretty, it never has been. But there's a purpose behind it, and I need for them to see that, before sending them toward the giant saws.

A couple of the pines emit no more than a sense of resignation. They know they're already doomed to die, might as well be today. A giant spruce toward the end of the line screams out in panic, while a smaller one, the one I fished out of the canal, is silent in confusion.

"I know, I know. Doesn't sound pleasant. And it isn't. But I'm here to tell you it's still going to be worth it."

I have their attention now. I give them an encouraging smile. "Just bear with me for a moment, okay?" I point to a second building. "This is where the larger trunks will be cut into firewood, and the smaller ones together with the branches will be cut into mulch. Yeah, doesn't sound very pleasant, but it's a good thing, honest."

Contemplating the line of beautiful trees in my care, I feel pride rising in my chest. "This means you still have a purpose, see? First, you were growing in the forest. Then, men came to cut you down and sell you for a profit. Then you were adopted by families and helped them create their version of the Christmas spirit. But even though they've now thrown you away, your path doesn't end here.

"The firewood's obvious, isn't it? You'll help some family keep warm next winter. That's an admirable purpose right there.

"And the mulch? It's gonna help make the city pretty. See, it's excellent for helping plants grow in a big city. Big pots of earth let trees grow amid the buildings, but if we just leave the earth exposed, it's gonna harden and sprout an impressive amount of weeds. If we spread the mulch, your remains, on top, it's a protective and nourishing layer, all in one!"

I make another pass down the line. They're contemplative. The large spruce seems proud she'll make lots of firewood. The small one from the canal is remembering a large potted tree he passed on his last trip with his hostess, how happy it had seemed despite the relatively small pot. He liked the idea of helping others grow.

As I signal to the sawmill workers to come get the trees, I let all my pride show on my face to give the trees a boost of confidence.

"I'm very proud of you all. You've grown into gorgeous trees that families wished to share their Christmas with, and you've done your work flawlessly. There's just one last task for you today, which will allow you to be part of something even bigger—the circle of life."

I shut up as the workers drag the trees away. A few years back, two of them overheard me talking to the trees, and they gave me a wide berth for the duration of our collaboration. I don't really care what they think, but want to avoid the trees having the last conversation they hear be a negative one.

Once they're all in the sawmill, I go to the back of my truck. Leaning up against the cab, the plastic tree is all alone.

"As you've probably gathered," I say with a soothing smile, "you don't get off here. Wouldn't be very effective as firewood or compost, I'm afraid." I slap the side of the truck. "But no worries. I've found a job for you, too. Follow me."

Two hours later, we bump down the road to a small cabin in the woods. My neighbor gave me the address; it's apparently a distant cousin of his.

When I exit the truck, a tall, lanky man comes out the front door, closing it behind him. His clothes are worn, but clean, and his face is filled with laugh lines.

"What can I do for you?" he asks as I walk up and shake his hand.

"Your cousin Lionel gave me your address," I say. "I'm hoping you can help me out."

He's wary, but nods for me to continue.

"I work for the city of Toulouse," I say. "I'm in charge of collecting old Christmas trees and getting them recycled."

The man shakes his head. "I'm sorry you've come so far for nothing. We don't have—"

"I know you don't." I smile to make sure he knows I'm in no way judging him for that fact. "But I have a spare."

I wave at my truck, where the little plastic tree is still waiting. "I've a plastic friend who, unfortunately, isn't eligible for recycling, and he's had a rough time of it this past year. I'm looking to find him a new home."

The man's eyebrows shoot up and he glances at my truck. "But…it's January."

I can tell he's interested, though. He's working hard to take care of his family and never break any rules. He couldn't afford to buy a tree, and according to his cousin, he won't even consider cutting down one of the trees in the forest he's living in. The forest isn't his, so it would be stealing.

"Sure." I shrug. "But who says you can only have a tree for Christmas? Most people have to throw them out because they start losing their needles, but a plastic tree? Could stand proud in the middle of the living room all year round."

He licks his lips as he deliberates. His eyes are on the truck, but they flicker back to his house from time to time.

"It's free?" he finally asks.

"Of course," I say. "You're helping me out, honestly. I get kind of attached to the poor things, and I couldn't stomach throwing him in the trash."

He meets my eyes. "Him?"

"Sure." I nod vigorously. "It's definitely a him. He'd probably be really happy if you named him, actually."

"Huh. All right." He chews on his lip some more. "I'll see what the kids think."

I wait outside as he disappears into the cabin for five minutes. I take the time to pull the little tree out of the truck.

"Here you go," I whisper. "This'll be your new home. I have it on good authority that there will be very little yelling here. And there are, like, three or four kids. Maybe you'll even be allowed to work all year round. How about that?"

Its scentless scent carries hope. And joy. And gratefulness.

"You're welcome, buddy. May your life be a long one."

The cabin door slams open, and four kids sprint out. The ages seem to range from two to ten, but they run up to the truck together, the bigger kids helping the smaller ones keep up.

Their eyes go wide when they see the tree.

"It's gorgeous!"

"It's covered in snow!"

"It's almost as tall as Papa!"

I help the father unload the tree and watch as the family brings it into their house. The mother watches from the kitchen window, a baby on her hip and tears in her eyes.

I nod a greeting, then get into my truck. It's almost night, and I need to make my rounds in the streets of Toulouse. The lost Christmas trees need me.

tHANk YOu

THANK YOU FOR reading *A Second Chance*. I hope you enjoyed it. And feel free to tell others about it if you did!

The inspiration for this story came when I walked home one night and saw an abandoned Christmas tree stuck in the frozen Canal du Midi. I felt bad for it. So I found a new home for it in this story.

If you liked the the story, you might want to check out some of my other books mentioned on the next page. It's mostly mysteries, but a few other genre short stories will pop up, too.

And don't forget that the first book of my *Tolosa Mystery* series, *The Red Brick Haze*, is available for free on my website.

R.W. Wallace
www.rwwallace.com

Also by R.W. Wallace

Mystery

The Tolosa Mystery Series
The Red Brick Haze (free)
The Red Brick Cellars
The Red Brick Basilica

Ghost Detective Shorts (coming soon)
Just Desserts
Lost Friends
Family Bonds
Till Death
Family History
Common Ground
Heritage
Eternal Bond
New Beginnings

Short Stories
Cold Blue Eternity
Hidden Horrors
Critters
Gertrude and the Trojan Horse
First Impressions
Let Them Eat Cake
Out of Sight
Two's Company
Like Mother Like Daughter

Fantasy (short stories)
Unexpected Consequences
Morbier Impossible
A Second Chance

Science Fiction (short stories)
The Vanguard

Lollapalooza Shorts
Quarantine
Common Enemies
Coiled Danger
Mars Meeting

Adventure (short stories)
Size Matters

About the Author

R.W. WALLACE WRITES in most genres, though she tends to end up in mystery more often than not. Dead bodies keep popping up all over the place whenever she sits down in front of her keyboard.

The stories mostly take place in Norway or France; the country she was born in and the one that has been her home for two decades. Don't ask her why she writes in English—she won't have a sensible answer for you.

Her Ghost Detective short story series appears in *Pulphouse Magazine*, starting in issue #9.

You can find all her books, long and short, all genres, on rwwallace.com.

www.ingramcontent.com/pod-product-compliance
Lightning Source LLC
LaVergne TN
LVHW051923060526
838201LV00060B/4158